MY PONY JACK

A Viking Easy-to-Read

By
CARI MEISTER

Illustrated by
AMY YOUNG

VIKING

VIKING

Published by Penguin Group

Penguin Young Readers Group, 345 Hudson Street, New York, New York 10014, U.S.A.

Penguin Group (Canada), 10 Alcorn Avenue, Toronto, Ontario, Canada M4V 3B2

(a division of Pearson Penguin Canada Inc.)

Penguin Books Ltd, 80 Strand, London WC2R 0RL, England

Penguin Ireland, 25 St Stephen's Green, Dublin 2, Ireland (a division of Penguin Books Ltd)

Penguin Group (Australia), 250 Camberwell Road, Camberwell, Victoria 3124, Australia

(a division of Pearson Australia Group Pty Ltd)

Penguin Books India Pvt Ltd, 11 Community Centre, Panchsheel Park,

New Delhi – 110 017, India

Penguin Group (NZ), Cnr Airborne and Rosedale Roads, Albany, Auckland, New Zealand

(a division of Pearson New Zealand Ltd)

Penguin Books (South Africa) (Pty) Ltd, 24 Sturdee Avenue, Rosebank,

Johannesburg 2196, South Africa

Penguin Books Ltd, Registered Offices: 80 Strand, London WC2R 0RL, England

First published in 2005 by Viking, a division of Penguin Young Readers Group

1 3 5 7 9 10 8 6 4 2

LIBRARY OF CONGRESS CATALOGING-IN-PUBLICATION DATA

Meister, Cari.

My pony Jack / by Cari Meister; illustrated by Amy Young.

p. cm.

Summary: Easy-to-read, rhyming text follows Lacy as she spends a day with her pony,
giving him exercise, grooming him, and feeding him oats and hay.

ISBN 0-670-05917-X (hardcover)

[1. Ponies—Fiction. 2. Stories in rhyme.] I. Young, Amy, ill. II. Title.

PZ8.3.M5514My 2005   [E]—dc22   2004021417

Manufactured in China

Set in Bookman

Reading level: 1.8

*For Benjamin, who loves the ponies—*C. M.

*For Zöe—*A. Y.

This is my pony.

His name is Jack.

He is brown and white.

His nose is black.

Jack has a halter.

It goes around his head.

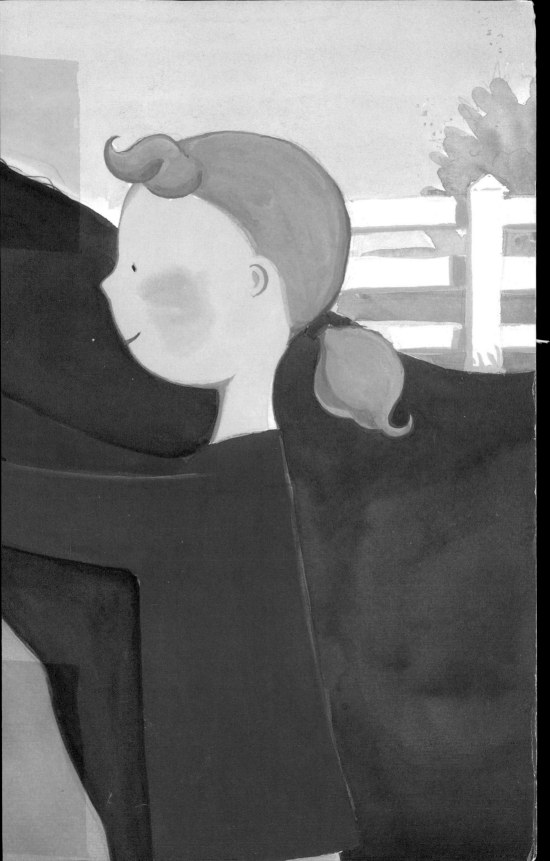

This is his lead rope.
It is bright red.

Walk on, Jack.

It is time to go in.

Back to the barn.

12

Whoa, out of the bin!

Hey Jack, let go!
You are a tease.

15

I will be right back.

Wait here, please.

This is the curry comb
Jack likes a lot.

I start with his neck,
his favorite spot.

I curry in circles.

That is the best way

to get out the dirt
Jack plays in all day.

LACY +
JACK

This is a soft brush.
It is for Jack's face.
Close your eyes, Jack.

This is a hoof pick.

It cleans out Jack's feet.

What a good boy, Jack!

Now you can eat.

Here are your oats.

Here is your hay.

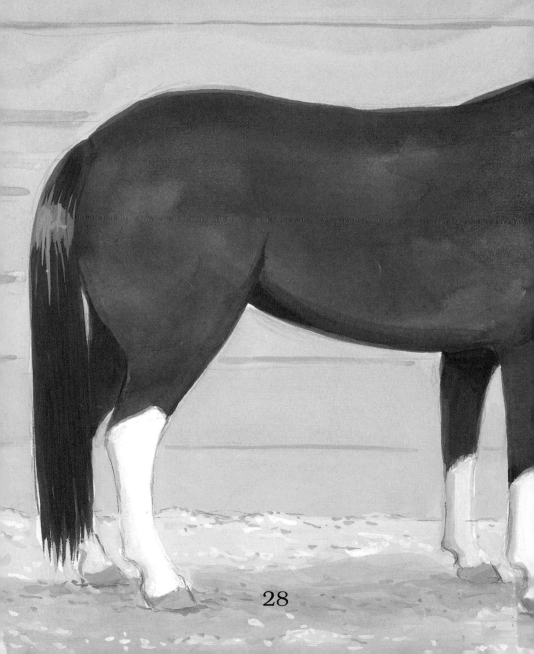

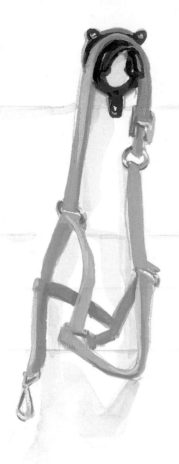

Here is a big kiss!
What a great day!

• PONY WORDS •

 **COMB**: a wide-toothed grooming tool used for a pony's mane and tail.

 CURRY COMB: a rubber grooming tool with rows of knobs used to remove dirt from a pony's coat.

 **FACE BRUSH**: an extra-soft brush made from goat hair used just for a pony's face.

 **HALTER**: a headpiece that a rope can be attached to in order to tie or lead a pony.

 HAY: grass that has been cut and dried to be used for a pony's food.

 HOOF PICK: a metal tool used to take stones and dirt from a pony's foot.

 **LEAD ROPE**: a rope with a metal clip that attaches to a halter, used to lead a pony.